GHOST BUMPS

by Michael J. Pellowski
illustrated by Don Robison

Published by Willowisp Press
801 94th Avenue North, St. Petersburg, Florida 33702

Copyright © 1987 by Willowisp Press,
a division of PAGES, Inc.

Printed in the United States of America   4 6 8 10 9 7 5 3   ISBN 0-87406-257-8

Luke was a warm-hearted little ghost who loved the summer sunshine. Snowy weather made Luke shiver and shake. That's why he flew south. But his friends were all back home now, and Luke was lonely.

One day Luke saw a sign for Dizzy World. VISIT OUR NEW HAUNTED HOUSE, the sign said.

"Oh, boy!" said Luke. "Ghosts! Maybe I can find a friend there."

The little ghost flew to the amusement park. He got a T-shirt and headed straight for the haunted house. It was old and crumbly. And it rumbled. Even to a ghost, the place looked scary.

The inside of the haunted house was dark and gloomy.

"Brr! It's c-c-cold in here," Luke sputtered as he turned blue. "I'm g-g-getting ghost bumps!"

Luke looked around. Suddenly an icy voice echoed out of the empty fireplace. "BOOO! What are you doing here?" the voice howled. And out popped a dusty old ghost.

"Freezing! That's what I'm doing here," said Luke with a shiver.

"Good! Haunted houses are supposed to send chills down your spine," bellowed the old ghost. Then he disappeared up the chimney.

"He wasn't very friendly," Luke mumbled as he went into the next room.

"ICK!" Luke stepped right into a big, sticky spider web.

"Yuck!" groaned Luke, looking around. The room was full of creepy cobwebs and big hairy spiders. "I hate spiders," Luke moaned as he hurried out the door.

In the hall was a group of ghosts. Maybe they'll be friendly, Luke thought.

The ghosts rattled chains and shrieked and screeched. Luke covered his ears. "What awful noise!" he complained.

"That's not noise," yelled a mean-looking ghost. "It's ghostly music."

Luke got away from the ghosts as fast as he could. He scrambled up a steep staircase into the attic.

"What a terrible place," Luke said with a shudder. "It's cold and damp. And the ghosts aren't friendly at all."

Suddenly Luke heard a terrible noise. CREAK! BANG!

The frightful noise made Luke jump. Then the room filled with bright light.

Luke moved slowly toward the light. Warm sunlight was streaming through a window. There, sitting in the sunshine, was a tiny witch.

Luke smiled. "You frightened me," he said.

"Oh, I didn't mean to frighten you," said the cute little witch. "My name is Wendy. I don't like cold, scary places. The sun is warm with the shutters open."

"Why don't you go outside?" Luke asked.

"I don't have any friends outside," the little witch replied.

Luke smiled a big, happy smile. "I'm Luke. I love sunshine, too."

Outside, Wendy and Luke had the warmest friendship of all. Luke turned toasty brown. And his ghost bumps? POOF! They disappeared like magic.